CW01213922

Great Uncle Bertie's Garden

DENNIS ROE

authorHOUSE

AuthorHouse™ UK
1663 Liberty Drive
Bloomington, IN 47403 USA
www.authorhouse.co.uk
Phone: UK TFN: 0800 0148641 (Toll Free inside the UK)
UK Local: 02036 956322 (+44 20 3695 6322 from outside the UK)

© 2021 Dennis Roe. All rights reserved.

No part of this book may be reproduced, stored in a retrieval system, or transmitted by any means without the written permission of the author.

Published by AuthorHouse 03/16/2021

ISBN: 978-1-6655-8471-5 (sc)
ISBN: 978-1-6655-8470-8 (hc)
ISBN: 978-1-6655-8472-2 (e)

Print information available on the last page.

Any people depicted in stock imagery provided by Getty Images are models, and such images are being used for illustrative purposes only.
Certain stock imagery © Getty Images.

This book is printed on acid-free paper.

Because of the dynamic nature of the Internet, any web addresses or links contained in this book may have changed since publication and may no longer be valid. The views expressed in this work are solely those of the author and do not necessarily reflect the views of the publisher, and the publisher hereby disclaims any responsibility for them.

# CHAPTER 1

The Magic Tree

Once, in a garden surrounded by thick green ivy close to a large wood full of huge trees and bushes, there lived a happy and wise old blackbird called Bertie with his lovely wife, Betty. All the birds loved him and called him "Great-Uncle Bertie". One day Bertie was sitting on a branch up in an old tree that stood at the top of the garden. His little spectacles were perched on the end of his beak. He was talking to his friend Cameron, who was a large, black, likeable crow.

Suddenly his grandson, Benny, arrived. He had spotted the nice people at the house they all called "Number 8" putting out food for the large variety of birds who visited the garden to enjoy the delights on offer.

"Come on, Grandad," whistled Benny. He got ready to fly into the garden to sample the fresh food.

"I am too old to be rushing down," replied Bertie. He stretched out his wings and snuggled back down to watch. "I remember being just like you when I was a young fledgling with your grandma. I always wanted to be first."

"You were young, Grandad?" Benny asked.

"Oh yes, Benny," he chuckled. "I can tell you stories."

By this time, other birds had arrived to listen to the stories that were going to be told.

"Go on, Grandad," Benny chirped as they settled on branches close by.

Bertie began. "Many years ago, my great-grandma told me about the time when all this area was just fields and trees as far as the eye could see. They didn't have all this lovely food put out for them. They had to search all around for worms and bugs."

"That sounds yummy," interrupted Reece and Rhianna Robin.

Close by, little Wilma and Willie Wren sat quietly listening. Wilma asked, "Did our mum and dad live nearby when the fields were here?"

Bertie smiled. "Oh yes. I even remember your grandparents. They had a lovely home in the deep undergrowth. But your parents were given a beautiful house by the friendly people over there." He pointed with his wing at Number 8. "Then slowly, little by little, more homes were put up all around the garden."

"Ooh," gasped Willie.

Sarah Song Thrush sat higher in the tree listening. "Oh, Bertie, your stories take me back to my childhood," she said softly.

Bertie continued, watching the attentive faces of the young birds. "I remember when a new feeder was brought into the garden. It was a lovely, covered area surrounded by water."

"We called it 'Lakeside'," chuckled Betty, with a wink of her eye.

More birds from around arrived to listen to the tales of the garden. Simon and Sally Sparrow flew down and asked about the small tree that stood at the other side of the garden.

"Ah yes," said Bertie. He glanced over to a green tree. "That is a very special tree! In fact, some birds used to call it magical." He glanced up to Sarah Song Thrush with a cheeky smile.

The young birds all sat with their beaks wide open.

"Magical?" asked Bianca and Billy Blue Tit together.

"Tell us more, please!" shouted Laura and Leo, the Long-Tailed Tits.

"Slow down, you two," whispered Sarah. "Bertie is getting to that now."

Bertie said, "When it starts to go dark, after all of you little ones are settling down for the night, something magical happens."

"What? What?" interrupted Benny.

"If you keep interrupting, we will never find out," grumbled Gemma and Gordon Goldfinch.

"Sorry," mumbled Benny.

Bertie went on. "Don't worry—I was young and impatient once. I couldn't wait to hear this from my mother and father either. But as it begins to go dark, something magical happens. The tree turns bright green, with little green sparkling stars all over it."

"*Wow*," gasped Callum Chaffinch, who had arrived with his brother Charlie and sister Clara to see what was happening and what all the commotion was about. They were swiftly followed by Barry and Brenda Bullfinch.

"Will the stars come on now?" asked Sally impatiently.

"Not yet, little one; it needs to start to go dark. But when it does, the tree will light up the garden with a bright green glow. It shines on to the small bushes down there. It also casts a light over the flowers that grow nearby," replied Bertie. "If you eat some food and get some rest, maybe your mums or dads will bring you back later to see. But only if you are good boys and girls."

"We will be good," they chirped as they flew away.

Later that evening, they all returned to see the special tree light up.

"Watch," said Bertie as the sun started to go down behind the trees in the wood. The magic tree suddenly lit up.

Staring with amazement, they said excitedly, "That's amazing! Look how it shines. It *does* look like the stars in the sky!"

Bertie looked around at the birds. It was clear that none of them wanted to leave. He sighed and said to them, "Anyway, little ones, it's time to settle down now. We can all meet again tomorrow, and then I will tell you more adventures from *Great-Uncle Bertie's Garden.*"

CHAPTER 2

The New House

The day started as normally as any other, with the sun gradually rising and lighting up all of nature's colours in the plants and trees around the garden. The sun awakened all the birds and other animals from their long sleep so they could enjoy the delights of what was about to surprise them.

It was also time for Brian and Belinda Bat to get ready to go to sleep. They'd had a busy night flying around searching for food before relaxing to get ready for the next night. In the distance could be heard a "Hoot, hoot!" from Ollie Owl. He was deep in the woods saying goodnight to everyone before he also settled down.

Bertie stretched out his wings, shook his tail, and waited for Benny and his sister, Beatrice, who had been at home the previous day, to arrive. When they arrived, they both sat on the opposite fence. Bertie, Benny and Beatrice watched as Molly and Max Magpie soared down into the garden with their brothers and sisters to get their first meal of the day before flying off to explore the nearby woods and surrounding gardens.

Molly and Max were being watched from the rooftop of Number 8 by Peter and Poppy Pigeon, who had been eyeing the juicy mealworms in the top food tray above Black Pole Tower. "It was the name Norman Nuthatch called it," Bertie said with a smile.

But earliest of all the birds were Sylvia and Steven Starling and their friends. They had already filled up on the lush goodies that had been on offer to start the day.

Bertie stretched, yawned, and said "Good morning" to his old and dear friends Sarah and Sammy Song Thrush. They flew on to the branch below. A little later Reece and Rhianna Robin woke up from the ivy bush, ate their first of many meals for that day, and swooped down on to a branch to hear more of Bertie's adventure stories.

After the other birds had arrived and found comfortable branches to sit on, Bertie began. "It was a warm day. The people at Number 8 had started to put up a new wooden feeding place."

Sammy laughed and said, "We call it 'Glamping Hall' because it looked like a wooden cabin that their aunt and uncle, who lived in a forest, had seen and described."

Bertie carried on with the story. "Yes, that's correct. It had a small house in the roof, and it stood proudly on top of a sturdy wooden stand. If the house had been big enough, Beatrice and Benny, your gran and I might have moved in," he joked. "Underneath the roof was a dry feeding area. We had lots of fun in all weathers there."

Bertie stopped for a second and asked the little birds if they wanted to hear something different. "Listen closely, children. If you settle down and be very quiet, you will hear a light tapping sound."

They all stopped to listen. As soon as it was quiet, they heard it: a tap-tapping sound echoing through the eerie silence. "What is that Grandad?" asked Beatrice nervously.

"Don't be frightened. It's only Walter and Winnie Woodpecker searching in the bark of the trees. They are looking for bugs and food to eat. If we are really lucky, sometimes they fly into the garden, showing their stunning black, white, and red feathers. They come to feast on the suet blocks hanging in the food holders in our trees," said Bertie.

"Will they?" asked Billy Blue Tit. "That would be so cool if they did!"

At that moment, Peter Pigeon flew down from the rooftops and started to act like a bully. He was trying to scare to the smaller birds. But the good people at Number 8 had a dog called Bella, and she rushed into the garden and chased off the naughty pigeon. He flew away fluttering and crying like a baby.

The little birds laughed at this. Bella would also chase Cyril and Cybil, the cheeky, bushy-tailed grey squirrels, if they were seen in the garden. They monkeyed around like tiny acrobats, hanging upside down. Sometimes they would hang by their back claws and tails to get to the delicious peanuts and suet that had been put out by the good lady.

"I remember one day Cyril tried to jump from the fence to get to some food hanging high on a washing line. 'Ready, set, go! Wheeeeee!' he shouted as he leapt across. Then, 'Help! Oh no, ouch!' he cried. Cyril fell on to the grass below with a bump. He had missed. He got up, looked around, and said, 'I am OK; it didn't hurt,' and then limped off." Bertie laughed.

Bella did not understand why the timid birds would not stay. She only wanted to play with her friends.

Bertie carried on with the story. "One day Mr and Mrs Nuthatch visited the garden to try the small, dainty peanuts inside a new peanut holder they had spotted from the trees in the wood."

Norman and Niamh Nuthatch looked at each other with beaks open and whispered, "That's our mum and dad." They both had big grins.

Sarah smiled and spoke to all the birds. "Come along you lot—time to leave. Let Bertie have something to eat. We will carry on tomorrow. We have all the time in the world to hear more adventures from *Great-Uncle Bertie's Garden*."

CHAPTER 3

The Day Out

Bertie woke early and waited for the birds to arrive to start the next story. When they were all there, he began. "One morning all the mums and dads were fluttering around twittering with excitement. The day they had been waiting for had arrived. They were going to go out and explore the wood nearby."

"Great-Uncle Bertie, what is it like over there?" asked Sally as the multicoloured leaves fell gently from the trees and twisted and swirled in the wind.

"Great-Uncle Bertie," started Reece, "why are the leaves that colour? I am sure they were green the other week."

Suddenly the wind blew through the trees, causing another shower of leaves.

"Grandad look out! The tree is falling!" Benny screamed

"It's OK, Benny," he replied. "This happens every autumn."

"What is autumn?" asked Beatrice.

"It is a special time of year. It is when the leaves all turn yellow, brown, and red and then fall all over the ground."

"Is that because the trees are tired?" she asked.

"No, not at all. It is when they start to get ready to sleep over the winter. Then, when the winter is over, they wake up and grow new green leaves and berries all over again," Bertie said.

It was early morning! We had all been down to the garden to eat. "Is everyone here!" someone shouted.

"Wait, wait," mumbled Suzie Sparrow as she tried to fit a little more food into her almost-full beak.

"Was that Sally's mum?" asked Wilma.

"It certainly was," came the reply. "We all flew deep into the wood towards the stream that gently trickled along, winding slowly between the trees and around the bend. Other birds had already arrived and were flapping around in the stream, splashing and wetting the others who were having a bath in the cool water."

"We do that in our own birdbath, don't we?" Billy Blue Tit looked a little puzzled.

"Yes, but not everyone is as lucky as us. Some have to use the stream or mucky puddles on the ground," answered Sarah.

Then suddenly—*whoosh*—Kerry Kingfisher flashed past, her bright-blue, turquoise, and orange feathers gleaming in the sun's rays.

"Erm, excuse me, but is there any food around here?" Suzie shouted as her tummy rumbled.

"I told you to eat something properly this morning," said Lenny Long-Tailed Tit, Leo's dad.

"I know, but I was too excited," she replied.

Kerry looked back with a small fish in her beak. "You can try to catch some more fish down there," she said as she flicked her head backwards.

"Oh no, not fish," said Suzie.

Kerry giggled, turned, and swiftly vanished around the bend in the stream. Then a small disagreement was heard.

"Let go! I said *let go*—it is mine!"

"No it isn't—it's mine!"

Two birds were squabbling over a worm they had found.

"There are more over there," one argued.

"Yes, but this is mine!"

They kept on squabbling. Suddenly they stopped and looked down. There was a movement in the leaves on the ground. Then they saw a small black pointed nose shuffling along through a sea of leaves. It was Horace Hedgehog.

"Oh hello," Horace said. "Who are you? And where do you come from?"

They pointed towards home. "Over there. We are on an adventure."

Horace continued. "Have you seen any juicy bugs for me? They will possibly be hiding in these leaves on the ground."

Lenny Long-Tailed Tit thought for a while, then told him, "Sorry, I haven't." He paused and looked around. "Can I ask you which tree you live in?"

Horace chuckled. "I don't live in a tree; I can't fly. I live down here on the floor in the brambles and hedges. Anyway, enjoy the rest of your day. Come back soon! Goodbye, all." Then he trundled away until he disappeared back into the leafy undergrowth.

As he left the birds could hear a noise coming from high above the tall trees. It was a strange honk, honk, honking sound. It got louder and louder, and when they looked up into the sky, they saw an amazing sight. There were lots of geese flying together in a very large *V* shape.

"Where are they all going?" asked the little birds as the geese slowly flew out of sight.

"Oh, they are flying to find warmer weather and look for food so they can feed their young babies after they are born," said Bertie.

It started to get a little darker, and they knew that the day was ending, so all the birds got ready to return home.

"I do hope you all had a good day out. It is time to go now," said Bertie. He looked around at the young birds, none of whom wanted the story to end, then quietly whispered, "Maybe we should go on our own day out when the weather gets warm, but now we have to get ready for sleep. When you come back, I can tell you more adventures from *Great-Uncle Bertie's Garden.*"

CHAPTER 4

The First Snow

It was a cold morning. Reece and Rhianna Robin had been pecking around on the ground and seed trays before flying into the thick green ivy that hung over the top of the fence to sit close together and snuggle up to keep warm.

"Brrrrr, why is it so cold today?" shivered Rhianna.

This woke up Bertie, who was having a snooze on a branch high up in the tree. "Oh, hello, little ones. You are up early. What seems to be the problem?" He stretched his wings, shook his tail feathers, and yawned. "It is very cold this morning, which means winter is nearly here. It could also be that snow is on its way."

Benny, who was sitting close by, looked puzzled. "Snow? What is snow?"

"Snow is when the rain high up in the clouds in the sky gets very cold and turns into light fluffy flakes that sparkle like tiny twinkling spiderwebs as they fall down," Bertie explained.

Benny looked across the garden and said, "Just like Suzie Spider's web on the big black archway over the gate down there?"

Sarah answered, "Yes, that's correct. Now settle down, children, and we will tell you more."

In the distance they heard voices saying "Wait, wait! We are on our way." Soon the other birds arrived and found branches to sit on. Some of them chirped eagerly as they waited to hear Bertie's stories.

"It was a cold morning, just like today," whispered Bertie. "We were woken by the sound of wind howling through the branches of the trees. It slowly began to snow—only lightly at first. It looked like tiny white feathers floating down from the sky. Then it started to get heavier and heavier until it began to cover the branches in the trees, the green grass, the magic tree, the houses, and all the stones in the garden. It looked like a large white fluffy blanket all around."

Sally Sparrow looked up and said in a quiet voice, "What happened to all the little flowers?"

Bertie carried on with the story. "The snow began to land softly on the flowers and leaves, causing some to bend over. Soon everything was white with the snow."

Simon thought to himself, then asked, "Were all the feeding areas still OK?"

Bertie looked down at the small bird, who was glancing around the garden. "All of the feeders were also covered with the snow. We had to hop around on the ground to see if we could find any bits of food left over until the people from the house came out to brush away the cold snow, then fill up all the feeding places for us with peanuts, seeds, and lots of other goodies. As soon as they finished, they went back indoors to sit and watch through the window. We all scrambled down to get some of the lovely food before the big greedy birds took it all. When we were done, we flew back up into our trees and huddled together for warmth."

"I bet it was freezing, just waiting around," replied Benny.

His grandma Betty Blackbird laughed. "We all sat around after we finished eating and looked down at the small prints which were made by your mums and dads as they hopped around in the snow in the garden."

While Betty was telling them all about the footprints, it started to snow again. Sammy Song Thrush stretched out his wing to try to catch one of the small snowflakes as it fell. Just as it landed on his wing, it disappeared. "Ooh, where did that go?" he asked.

Sarah giggled. "If it continues like this, it will cover all the garden, not just your wing."

Jamie and Judy Jay Bird stood on top of the nearby greenhouse and watched as the cold white snowflakes slowly drifted down from above. The rusty red tree in the middle of the garden tried to stand proud, its crimson leaves still showing as the rest of the garden vanished under the snow.

Laura Long-Tailed Tit looked across the garden and noticed some water that seemed to be dripping down from the edges of the roof but was not falling on to the ground. "Why is that water hanging off the house but not falling?"

Bertie turned around to see what Laura was looking at. "Ah, those are icicles, Laura. They occur when the cold freezes the water droplets to make a pointed spike that only melts when it gets warmer."

The snow continued to fall and cover the garden just like Bertie had described. Peter and Poppy Pigeon fluttered down into the garden. Their flapping wings scattered the light covering of snow, making it look like more snow was falling again. They looked for more food, then flew away again to settle down.

The day started getting colder. Bertie looked around at the young shivering birds and told them, "Go and get something to eat and also get a drink of water. If this weather gets any colder, our water may freeze, and you will have to peck through the ice to get more. Don't forget, children: huddle together and fluff up your feathers—it will help you keep warm."

The birds flew down to eat and drink before returning home to get comfortable. They were excited because they knew that very soon they would hear more adventures from *Great-Uncle Bertie's Garden.*

CHAPTER 5

The New Fountain

The sun shone brightly in the garden, the sky was clear and blue, and all the birds were enjoying a hot summer's day. Some of the birds who were very warm had gone searching for shade in the trees and bushes.

Benny flapped his wings, trying to cool himself down, and said, "Why is it so hot?"

Bertie looked up and said, "Come over here, you two," to Benny and Beatrice. "I will tell you about a day when it was hotter than this. A new fountain had arrived in the garden. It was put in over one of our birdbaths over there. Some of us were just like you, trying to shelter under the new leaves that had filled all of the branches on the trees. By this time the surrounding fruit trees had started blossoming. Some had starting to grow berries and small fruits. The nice lady had planted some new small plants, and lots of the flowers had started to bloom. The yellow daffodils, tiny bluebells, and white snowdrops were showing all their vibrant colours. Summer had almost arrived."

By this time the other birds had settled down to listen. Bertie continued. "We watched as Bronwyn and Brian Bee buzzed around, in and out of the beautiful flowers and fruit trees, gathering lovely nectar to take back to their hive. This is how bees start to make honey."

"What about the fountain?" asked Simon Sparrow.

"It was a special fountain. The more the sun shone, the higher the fountain squirted, making it look like a tiny rain shower into the bowl."

Sarah joined and explained, "On hot days, we could have a drink of clear water and cool down under the water cascading down from the fountain. Different birds from other gardens and from all over the wood came to see what all the giggling and splashing was about. They watched as the little birds and some big birds as well all played around."

Willie Wren looked at Bertie and said, "We remember you telling us about the birds in the wood who splashed about in the stream."

Wilma said, "Yes, but ours is much better, isn't it?"

Sarah answered, "Yes, it certainly is."

Bertie told them, "We all watched, perched in the trees, as the nice people from Number 8 set the fountain up, then filled up the food areas before going inside to sit and watch us through the big window. We couldn't wait to go down to explore."

As Bertie spoke, Cyril and Cybil Squirrel kept peeping over the fence to check that Bella was not outside, then sneaking in to get some nuts and fruit to hide in the wood and next door's garden to eat later.

Steve Starling watched them and said, "I once saw Cyril take some pebbles from the garden, thinking they were peanuts. His sister didn't tell him they weren't; she just laughed at him."

Bertie looked around the tree and continued with the story. "One day when the sun started to go down, the lovely lady came out and turned on some lights in our tree. They were all different colours. She also turned on some round white lights hanging along the fence, around the gate, and over the archway that looked like little bubbles. Their light shone on to the wind chimes, which made gentle ringing sounds as the breeze made them swing around. They also lit up Suzie Spider's web. Their light caught the strands and made them glisten. It looked like the cold frost had come back. Even the white weeping willow tree lit up like a silver waterfall."

The birds chirped and cheeped to each other until Bianca Blue Tit tilted her head and said, "Listen, everyone. Great-Uncle Bertie, what is that noise?"

Bertie listened. It was like a humming noise. "Don't be afraid—it is just some cars and lorries that go very fast on the busy roads in the distance, way over there, over the houses and wood. They can be noisy and very dangerous, so we never go over there. People use cars and lorries to go to various places because they don't have wings like we do." Bertie flew down to the birds, who were all chattering noisily, and said, "Shh, children. I want to tell you about the time a new family arrived at our garden. Guess who it was? It was Gordon and Gemma's grandparents."

Gemma flapped her wings with excitement and pride. Bertie waited a second, then said, "They moved into one of the birdhouses over there. She had laid some eggs, and after all the chicks hatched they needed lots of food and rest so when they grew up they could play around in the garden. We all had to be very quiet until they started to fly around."

Just then Betty appeared and said, "Let's get ready for home now, and on our next gathering, maybe we will be able to hear more adventures from *Great-Uncle Bertie's Garden*."

CHAPTER 6

The Rainy Day

Rain dripped steadily on to Gordon Goldfinch's beak as he sat beside his sister, Gemma, sheltering under the green leaves.

Gordon groaned. "Will this rain ever stop? We cannot play in the garden with our friends, and we probably will not hear any more stories."

Bertie heard this from his branch high up in the wet tree. He flew down and sat close to them, shook his feathers and tail, and said, "Don't be sad. This reminds me of the time it rained for many days. Parts of the garden had large puddles. The stream I had told you about flooded, and it flowed through the wood very quickly."

As Bertie was speaking, the other birds arrived, ignoring the rain to listen to his stories. Bertie looked around, smiled, and continued. "The rain was soaking all the trees. We had no chance of having fun. Even the squirrels stayed at home in their dreys. It rained harder and harder until it looked like a mist had come down over the entire garden, making it difficult to see the other side."

Clara Chaffinch asked, "What did you all do?"

Bertie smiled. "Gradually it began to ease. Then it stopped, and the sun slowly started to appear through the black clouds as they rolled away to leave a clear blue sky."

Benny glanced up. "What is that over there, Grandad?"

They all looked over to see what he was looking at. There was a large multicoloured arch spreading across the sky over the houses and trees.

Sarah replied, "That is called a *rainbow*. It is a sign to tell us the rain is going away and some nice weather will soon be here."

Bertie nodded. "Your parents didn't like the rain, but after it had gone they played in the birdbaths, splashing around and giggling." Bertie leaned over to Sally Sparrow and said, "Your grandparents were laughing at your dad as he played in the water. He didn't like the rain, but he told them this was different—this was fun.

"Spring had arrived. The dull garden, which had lost all of its colour over the winter months, was now beginning to show green shoots on the flowers, bushes, and trees. They had woken up from their winter sleep to bloom again and produce lovely colours that brightened up the garden and surrounding wood. Your parents would sit high up in the trees in the wood and watch the nice people put in new colourful plants to fill the spaces."

Rhianna Robin whispered, "Look! Bella is running up and down the garden, swishing her black-and-white tail from side to side and barking at the raindrops falling from the trees. She is so funny."

Reece glanced at his sister. "Please be quiet; we can watch her after the story."

Bertie said, "Don't worry. Anyway, the garden had started to show signs of strawberries, blackcurrants, cherries, and other fruits, just like the previous years, giving your parents lots of tasty treats."

Bianca Blue Tit looked across to the fruit trees. "Can we eat the fruits when they come?"

"Oh yes. They will be very tasty," said Sarah.

Bunty Butterfly fluttered by, the sun shining on her beautiful coloured wings.

"Hello, Bunty," Bertie called.

"Hello, everyone. Sorry, I can't stop; I have just spotted some lovely flowers. I will see you all soon. Goodbye!" She rapidly flew away.

Bertie told everyone to settle down and started again. "I remember when we all started to look around for somewhere to build new nests. We collected twigs and other items to make them comfortable. Some of your mums and dads were looking at the new houses that were put up around the garden. The people at the house had put out fur from Bella's coat and soft feathers from Ruby the pet parrot, who lives inside the house. These made our nests nice and warm and snug for the chicks after they hatched."

Gabrielle Great Tit smiled and said, "I think my mum and dad have started to make a nest in the nice green birdhouse over there."

Sarah spoke softly. "In a few weeks lots of you will have little brothers and sisters to look after, and someday you can tell them Bertie's tales."

The birds cheered. "We can't wait!"

It began to go dull again. Across the darkening sky a great flash of light lit up all around, "followed by a large CRASH!"

Brenda Bullfinch cowered. "What was that Great-Uncle Bertie?"

"It's called thunder and lightning. It means another rainstorm is coming. It is time for all of you to take cover around the garden and in your trees in the wood."

As it began to rain and the birds started flying away, they could hear Bertie shouting, "Take care, everyone! Who knows, someday I may have more adventures from *Great-Uncle Bertie's Garden.*"

Printed in Great Britain
by Amazon